# Table of Contents

Poetry is a special form of writing that speaks to the heart as well as to the mind.
You can like a poem for what it says (that's the mind part) and you can like it for how it makes you feel (that's the heart part).
Poets create word pictures using "sensory" details that describe sights, sounds, smells, tastes, and other physical feelings. Poets also create special word pictures by comparing different things.
Poetry is a wonderful thing!

# DEDICATED TO
My family

# I Am From...

I am from the mistful snow in Minnesota

I am from the backyard

I am from Grace being so kind

I am from my family I love my family

I am doodling I love drawing art and painting

I am free and safe

## I am Rowyn Helker

# Hockey practice

Click

Clack

Goes the sticks

Bang!

Bang!

Goes the pucks against the boards

Whoosh

Whoosh!

Goes the people passing me

Screeech

Screeech!

Goes my skates

Bunnies

Fluffy                              Cute

Hopping              Bouncing                    Eating

Animal          Pet                    Mammal              Rabbit

Hopping                    Cuddling                  Drinking

Furry              A fluff ball

Baby

My Dad is like a beaver because he is always working hard on our house and for our family.

My Mom is like a cuddly koala because she cuddles with me a lot.

I'm a rabbit because I'm quiet when I'm not around people that are my family or friends. I'm also shy.

My brother is like a dog because he is loving and caring. He makes people cheer up!

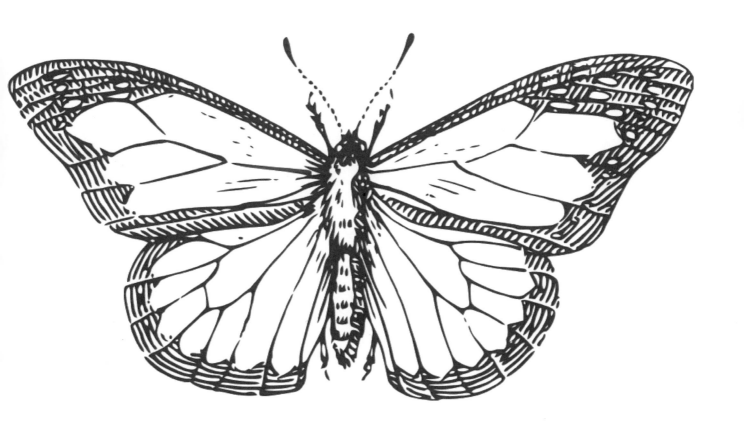

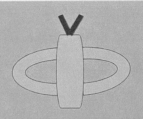

# Butterflies!

Butterflies are nice

As nice a as cup of tea.

Very beautiful!

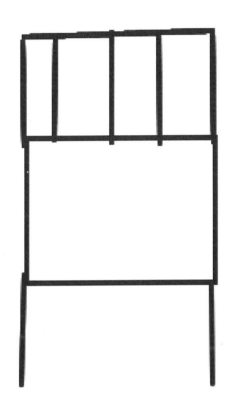

# The unfair chair

There once was a chair

That was always unfair

Never letting the other chairs play

Sadly they had to play with clay

Giving them a deep stare

Callie clapped casually as she collided

# ALL ABOUT THE AUTHOR

Hi! My name is Rowyn Helker. I live in Rogers, Minnesota. I love hockey, animals, my family, and much more! I'm in 4th grade. I have one sibling named Van. My favorite types of books are history, mystery, poetry, and diaries! My favorite book is Dork Diaries by Rachel Renee Russell.

# This would make a great gift!

For a limited time, your child's one-of-a-kind book is available to order for family and friends!

## Share the smiles
and preserve childhood memories for a lifetime . . .
Order your one-of-a-kind gift today!

Written and Illustrated by
Mrs. Austermiller's First Grade Class 2013-2014

Copies starting at
## only: $19.95
+ shipping and handling

## Perfect for:
- Grandparents
- Mother's or Father's Day
- Holidays and birthdays
- Your child's keepsake box

## Ordering is fast and easy:

1. Go to **studentreasures.com/ordercopies**

2. **Enter the 6-7 digit PIN number found in the center of the back cover of your child's book**

1345 SW 42nd Street
Topeka, KS 66609
800-867-2292

Dear Parent,

We think you will agree that this is an exceptional book. A tremendous amount of time and effort went into creating this book. The students learned a great deal about the publishing process while they improved their vocabulary and writing skills. Plus, being a young published author gives a sense of pride and accomplishment.

Your child is very fortunate to have a teacher who provides innovative activities that enhance the educational experience. We know you and your child will cherish this lifetime keepsake.

# Enjoy!

Studentreasures® Publishing

Studentreasures.com

# 587611LV00005B/5

# TBLUEENDS:COLORSTD70

# CASE **MATTE**

611LVX00141BA - 687611LVX00141BA [ 1 : 1 ]

687611LV00005B*

OOK

TCO7019_LG          CONTAINS: COLOR

# REWORK

ana McCarthy

te: _____

me: _____

me: _____

nes: _____

Promise Date: 19-MAY-21 (WED)

687611LV*

## Batch 687611LV00005B

| 687611LVX00141BA | CS05240182TRP | Mrs. Hammerschmidt & Mrs. Dockend |
|---|---|---|
| CASE | 8.50X11.00 | 24    <A>   0.375    MATTE |

Please note this is a Transient Print Book

# THE MIGHTY MOUNTAIN AND THE MUSTARD SEED

By Candace Alford

Illustrated by Kate Witt

Text Copyright © 2021 Candace Alford
Illustrations Copyright © 2021 Kate Witt
All illustrations created with Art Markers and Photoshop.

Formatting by Travis D. Peterson of Launch Mission Creative
**launchmissioncreative.com**

Self-Published 2021
Assisted by At Home Author

ISBNs:

978-1-7365314-0-2 ǀ Hardcover
978-1-7365314-1-9 ǀ Softcover

Learn more about Candace Alford at:
**comealivewithcandace.com**

For Lucas, Evelyn, and Jane, my little mustard seeds,
who move me in mighty ways every single day.
Love Always, Mom


For Marcus, my mighty mountain and better half,
who keeps me grounded, encourages me, and never ceases to amaze me.
Thank you for a love that only grows deeper and stronger
with each passing day.

Way up high, through the clouds, lived the Mighty Mountain. He was the tallest and boldest - no bigger mountain could be found.

At the tippity-top of the Mighty Mountain lived a family of mustard seeds.

Each morning as the sun would peek out above the horizon, the Mighty Mountain would slowly wake from his lazy slumber.

On the other hand, the small family of mustard seeds would be up by morning's first glow, working hard. Even though they were small, the mustard seeds believed they could do BIG things!

One beautiful day, after a long morning of lounging, the Mighty Mountain yawned as the sun hit high noon. "Perfect time for a nap!" he said, finishing up his yawn.

As he settled in for a snooze, he was quickly disturbed by the pitter-patter of teeny, tiny feet.

Cracking open one eye to find the source of the annoyance, he squinted and strained his eyes. Finally, he spotted the youngest member of the little mustard seed family.

"You sure make a lot of noise for such a little seed!"
he bellowed, irritated by the interruption.

The seed stood between the eyes of the Mighty Mountain,
grinning from ear to ear.

"I'm sorry for the inconvenience, Mr. Mountain, sir. But I must work extra hard, as I am the smallest in my family. A job that takes the others one day, takes me two, or sometimes three days to do!"

The Mighty Mountain let out an arrogant, "Humph!" and barked, "Too bad you're not as big and mighty as a mountain! All I have to do is sit here, and people marvel at me!"

Wide-eyed, the tiny seed was astonished, "You do nothing all day?"

Proud of himself, the Mighty Mountain said,
"Yes, and I am still the biggest and strongest,
there is no one more mighty than me!"

Thinking through this new-found knowledge, the tiny seed said deep from his heart, "Are you sure that's true?"

Confused, the Mighty Mountain grumped, "What do you mean?"

"Well, you are the biggest," said the seed.
"But how sad, that you'll never really grow!"

Befuddled, the Mighty Mountain scoffed, "Why must I grow? I'm the biggest and strongest. Everybody knows!"

With sad little eyes, the tiny seed said, "You are mighty in size, sir, that much is true! But what about your faith, Mr. Mountain?"

Not liking the challenge, the Mighty Mountain roared, "What is this faith you dare say I need? I'm the Mighty Mountain, you're just a tiny, little seed!"

"Yes, I am small, but I know of someone even more mighty than you!"

"Impossible!" fired back the Mighty Mountain in rage. "Who could be more mighty than me?"

In a humble tone the little mustard seed confirmed, "Well it's God! Jesus said, "I tell you the truth, if you have faith even as small as a mustard seed, you could say to this mountain, 'Move from here to there,' and it would move." [Matthew 17:20]

You see, it's not your gigantic size or that I'm a tiny seed that reveals the power inside of me.

It's my trust in God and not myself that makes everything possible!

Closing his eyes, the tiny young seed let out a sigh and fell to his knees.

"Dear God,
Reveal Your mighty power today!
There is nothing too big!
No request is too small.
I have faith in You, Father,
please use every little bit of me!"

And what happened next, you wouldn't believe.
That mighty mountain, the biggest of all, was lifted and
moved by the tiniest seed.

Up high in the sky, the Mighty Mountain stared in fascination at the tiny young seed holding him in the air.

In that very second, everything the mustard seed had said became perfectly clear.

From that moment on the Mighty Mountain grew, not in size, but in his heart, as he knew the Truth. That tiny young seed did a brave thing that day, he put his faith in the Lord and faced the mightiest mountain. His boldness in truth proved that absolutely nothing is impossible with God!

If you ever feel like a small mustard seed up against a mighty mountain,
just remember God's Word, and join me as I pray:

"Heavenly Father, I believe in You!
That no matter my size or the mountains I face,
I know that your love always wins, every single day!
Use me, God, to share your truth with each and everyone I meet.
Help me to be bold and strong and live it out in my life,
so there is no question of your goodness and grace!
Thank You, Lord, for who You are and Your never-ending love for me!
In Jesus' Name, Amen."

Now go and be brave like the tiny mustard seed!
Move mighty mountains by faith so others may come to believe!

To God be the glory!

Matthew 17:20 (NIV),
"You don't have enough faith," Jesus told them.
"I tell you the truth, if you have faith even as small as a mustard seed,
you could say to this mountain, 'Move from here to there,'
and it would move. Nothing would be impossible."

Did you know that a mustard seed is one of the smallest seeds in the world, measuring 1 to 2 millimeters in size?  The tiny seed will grow into a large bush that can be more than 30 feet tall!

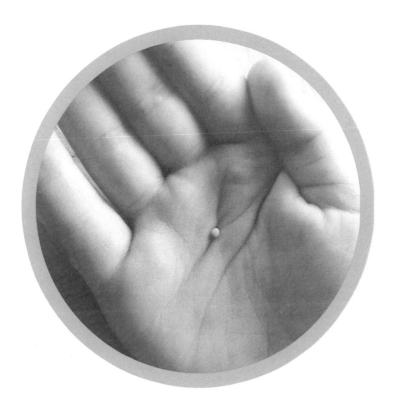

Jesus uses this special seed for numerous stories in the Bible to show that the power of God can be found in the smallest of things.

Candace Alford developed her passion for writing as a young girl but recently began recording areas of growth in her own life as well as those of her inspirational children. Her desire to share her writing stemmed from personal triumphs only achieved through her Lord and Savior.

Graduating with a Bachelor of Science, she double majored in Mass Communications and Journalism from Wayne State College. She wears many hats as a Mom, Farm Wife, Ministry,Enthusiast, Fitness Instructor, Writer, Motivational Speaker, and newfound Blogger, Come Alive with Candace.

Candace currently resides with her husband, Marcus, and their three children, Lucas, Evelyn, and Jane on their three-generation family farm where she is fortunate to fulfill the calling to be a stay-at-home Mom and homeschool. She loves baking, being outdoors, music, quoting movies and shows, being surrounded by loved ones, and meeting new people.

Kate Witt creates art with a variety of mediums including acrylic, ink, charcoal, pencil, marker, and Photoshop. She has been creating art all her life and began working professionally in 2002.

Kate attended the University of Nebraska where she earned a degree in Fine Art. Upon graduation in 2003, Kate spent the next six years traveling and living between Nebraska, Nantucket Island, Spain and Ireland. A rich array of experiences has brought her back to the Mid-west where she now sculpts, paints and designs in her studio. Recently, Kate has begun painting large outdoor murals.

Kate teaches art at Burke School in Burke, South Dakota where she resides with her husband and four children.
This is Kate's second book.

CPSIA information can be obtained
at www.ICGtesting.com
Printed in the USA
LVRC080749210521
687891LV00032B/43